DANIEL
AND THE
DREAM

CANAAN GILBERT

ISBN-13: 979-8-3462-9994-3

CONTENTS

Acknowledgments

Thank you to my parents for editing my books, and I thank you for buying this book. While this is fiction, it contains Biblical truths. I hope it encourages you to read the Word of God.

Prologue

The Fallen Kings

Daniel King was an 8-year-old kid who lived in Orlando, Florida with his parents, David and Sarah King. His parents loved God and went to church every Sunday to learn the Word. Daniel enjoyed his time at church looking through his beautiful Bible to find every verse that hinted of the Messiah and thought about how they lined up to what Jesus did. Daniel loved his time at church just as his parents did.

Daniel had a best friend, Conner Higgins, who went to the same church as him. Conner loved just talking and playing card games with him at Daniel's house on game nights. But when Daniel turned 8, Conner moved to Sacramento, California to be near family. Daniel was unable to talk with Conner for a long time. Daniel was deeply saddened by this, and his parents were, too, because they were friends with Conner's parents. They knew that Daniel didn't have a friend to talk and learn with.

Daniel's father had an upcoming business trip in Sacramento, so Daniel's mom decided to tag along, and while there, they would check on the Higgens family. Daniel couldn't go because of his basketball championship, so they left him with their good friends, the Mitchells.

"We will be back in a few days," his parents both told him the day they left.

On the way to the airport, his parents were killed in a car accident. It was the same day Daniel's team won the championship. Daniel grieved.

On the day of the funeral, he sat near their graves with his Bible and threw it onto the ground and left it there out of anger.

That day, Daniel changed and blamed God for his parents' deaths.

Chapter 1

The King All Grown Up

Daniel is now a 28-year-old shop employee at Walmart in Perdido Key, Florida. He lives in a rundown apartment building. He still goes to church on Sundays, but the only reason he goes is so that when he is with a group of other people, whom he calls his "friends," he can be the antagonist of the group.

Daniel likes to talk about all the little details in the Bible that he thinks don't really work, and he never explains the real reason for his strange dislike of Christianity. The people he normally sits with at church actually do consider Daniel to be a friend. They find that he can be funny, even when he is being a little annoying. They always expect their tall friend to be walking in late, as he usually is, and to hear him talk about silly things that make no sense to him. Even though they know what he is trying to do – to make them see that their faith is dumb – they still give him a place to talk. They try their best to help him in any ways they can.

Daniel is always trying to make them understand

that to him Christianity is wrong, but most of the things he says don't make a lot of sense! He just comes off sounding angry. His attempts to move his friends from their faith has not worked. Their faith was strong!

David has had a very hard life after the death of his parents. He's been evicted two times for what he says is "no reason that he knew of." But there were always reasons.

Every day he missed his parents and Conner. He never got to see him again after he moved away to California.

One night, Daniel was invited by his church friends to dinner at a fancy restaurant not too far from him. After all the times they had listened to him, now they wanted a chance to talk to him.

Chapter 2

The Dinner

Daniel was getting ready for his dinner with his "friends" to discuss some important topics. Daniel didn't know what they wanted to discuss with him, but he was ready to find out and challenge whatever they had to say.

Daniel left his apartment and decided to walk there because it was just a few blocks away. When he got there, he was surprisingly about 20 minutes early. He had to wait just a little until his "friends" finally arrived.

They all sat down for their discussion, but first they had to order.

"I will get the large double-stack cheeseburger please," one of Daniel's "friends" said to the waiter.

"I will order the double-stack supreme with no tomatoes," Daniel said.

"OK, let's talk!" one of Daniel's "friends," Richard, said.

"Talk about what?" Daniel asked.

"We have been discussing it when you weren't

around, and we decided that if you don't stop insulting our religion, we will have to ask you to leave our group," Richard answered.

"Why? Is it because you guys don't like being proved wrong about your religion?" Daniel pridefully asked.

"No," Richard replied. "It's because you aren't just insulting us, you are insulting your Maker and our Maker! If you won't stop, we will all have to have a meeting with our lead pastor."

"You guys are crazy!" Daniel argued. "You're not as welcoming and loving as you claim to be."

"We're not crazy," Richard said. "We just have high standards for how we should all treat each other."

Another one of Daniel's "friends" looked very annoyed and finally interjected, "Richard, stop trying to accommodate him. Daniel, you need therapy!"

The other restaurant guests near them noticed them talking, and they tried to look away from them because it was making them uncomfortable. Daniel noticed it and decided to leave his "friends" and go home.

When he was leaving the restaurant, the waiter quickly gave him his food. Daniel went home, ate his food alone and then decided to get some sleep.

Chapter 3

The Dream

Just after midnight, Daniel woke up suddenly. He saw a light shining around his bedroom door. Daniel thought he left a light on in the dining room, but he certainly did not!

When he opened the bedroom door, he didn't see his dining room at all. He saw a forest around him, and the source of the light was nowhere to be seen. What he did see instead was a cloaked figure in black and red standing in the distance, but not too far away from Daniel.

"Who are you?" Daniel wondered aloud.

The cloaked figure said something that would linger and creep around in Daniel's head for many years to come.

"My name is Lucien. Who are you?" the cloaked figure asked.

When Daniel heard the words, he felt a shiver down his spine. For some reason, the name sounded familiar, but Daniel couldn't quite figure out why it was familiar.

Lucien took off his cloak and revealed that he was

something more evil than anything Daniel has ever seen. He revealed that he had two horns on his head, his skin was dark red, and he had two giant wings protruding from his back.

"People from your world might use other names to refer to me," Lucien said. "Why are you here? Tell me now!"

"I don't know," Daniel said. "I just opened my bedroom door, and then I was here. Please don't hurt me."

"I might spare you if you come to me and do not go to the Son," Lucien replied.

Daniel felt even more fear, but he knew he could not give in to it.

"I would rather see who this Son guy is than go walking with you," Daniel said. "All I want right now is to go home."

Chapter 4

Lucien

"Well, then you have a death wish because I will kill you before you can even leave this road," Lucien said. "Unless you join me, you will die. Which one do you want? Life or death?"

"I would rather die than go with you." Daniel said.

"That's a good choice!" someone who came out of the shadows of the forest interjected.

It was another cloaked figure, but from what Daniel could tell, this cloaked entity was human. The colors of the cloak were black and blue instead of black and red like those Lucien wore. Daniel felt a sigh of relief because he wasn't the only human there, but Daniel didn't completely trust this man quite yet.

"Don't fear, civilian, I do not work for him, and I have a sword for you," the cloaked human said. "Do you know how to use a sword?"

"No, I have never held a sword in my life!" Daniel said, exasperated. He felt kind of dumb for not knowing how to use a sword especially in this moment when knowing how to wield a sword would come in handy.

"Well, you will have to do your best," the cloaked human said. "Do you know how to play baseball? The skills of a bat would come in handy."

"Actually, yeah!" Daniel replied happily. "I played baseball with my friend in the backyard!"

Daniel was handed the sword and ran as fast as he could toward Lucien. He swung his sword around but missed his target by a lot.

"Ummm, I have an idea," the cloaked human said. "Keep your eyes on the target. Don't lose focus."

"OK!" Daniel said.

Daniel swung again and still missed. The momentum from the swing put him on unsettled ground, which crumbled beneath his feet. Daniel began to fall but caught the edge of the ground with his arms.

"You know," Lucien said. "I think I should leave so I can give you guys some time so you both can get more prepared."

Lucien flew away.

The cloaked human ran to help Daniel, and when he grabbed his hands, he saw Daniel's face clearly.

"Daniel?" the man asked.

Then Daniel saw the man's face.

"Conner?" Daniel asked, shocked. "What are you doing here?"

Chapter 5

The Reunion

"Don't you mean what are YOU doing here? Did you get stuck here as well?" Conner asked.

"I don't know! I just got here and the first thing I see is that monster!" Daniel said.

"You know, it doesn't matter right now," Conner replied. "What does matter is that you're safe. I'm so happy to see you!"

"Yeah," Daniel agreed. "I haven't seen you in about 20 years. I missed you so much. I do want to know, though, how on earth you got here just like I did!? This has to be a dream. It can't be real."

"I met some people here a long time ago," Conner answered. "They told me that there are a small number of people on earth who can have dreams that actually become real. People have died from it. The people who told me eventually died in here, too. I think that guy you already met is to blame."

"A dream that can become real?" Daniel asked.

"Yes," Conner said. "Daniel, we got here in a dream, but… It's real to us now."

"What happens if you die here?" Daniel asked.

"You mean, do you also die back home?" Conner said. "That man you just fought sure seems to believe so. That's why he's always trying to turn us or kill us."

"How long have you been in here?" Daniel asked.

"To be honest, I don't know," Conner said. "You lose track of time very quickly in here."

"Do you know how to get out of this… dream?" Daniel asked.

"Yes and no," Conner said. "I know who can help us get out of here, but I don't know how He does it."

"Have you ever met him?" Daniel asked.

"Not yet," Conner said. "Mainly because every time I tried to get to Him, I was almost killed by Lucien and his henchmen. The thing is, I know some people who can help us. I think they can help us get out of this place."

"And *this* place is what exactly?" Daniel asked.

"This place is called the Kingdom of the Son, or Takiro," Conner said.

Daniel felt a tinge of excitement at hearing the name.

"Well," Conner started. "Let's roll!"

Chapter 6

The Adventure Begins

Conner led the way. Daniel's mind was full of questions as he trailed behind Conner as they trekked through the desolate, dry land.

"Why is this place called the Kingdom of the Sun?" Daniel asked. "Do the people here worship the sun and moon and stars or something?"

"No, not sun like the giant ball of gas in the sky," Conner said. "The Son. Son like a boy child."

"Well, who is he, this son guy? What is he?" Daniel asked.

"Well, I don't know if there is an answer to that question," Conner said. "I have asked these questions to the people I have met here, and I have heard their ideas on who and what He is. Some said He was a human, and others said He was a dazzling, bright shining man who helped the Protectors every now and then. Most people I've met said He shined like the sun, so much that they couldn't see His face."

"Who are the Protectors?" Daniel wondered aloud.

"They are a group of men and women who help and give hope to the villages that were burned down by Lucien," Conner said. "The Protectors are led by 12 men who knew the Son best. He helps people like me and you get out of this… place. We have to go to the Son's Castle to find the Son, but we can't find the Son without the Protectors."

They traveled for hours, and eventually the dry, barren land slowly transformed into a thriving forest land. Along the way, Conner taught Daniel how to better use a sword. As night began to fall, they set camp next to a lake so that in the morning they could have some fish to eat.

Daniel had a miserable sleep. He was terrified of Lucien and wondered if he would get to leave this place. He was also still aggravated about his conversation with his "friends" the night before. He was also terrified of his past and the beliefs he had given up. He didn't quite know why, but he felt like the reason he was stuck in the Kingdom was because of his unbelief, almost as if he was being punished.

Daniel didn't want to change his ways because he still had hatred in his heart of which he refused to let go.

Chapter 7

Conner's View

The next morning, Conner woke before Daniel and prepared his fishing rod to catch breakfast.

While he didn't want to admit it to Daniel, Conner was a little nervous about going to the Son's Castle because he had tried going there unsuccessfully many times. Every previous attempt, he would be forced to retreat because of Lucien and his army.

Conner was happy to see Daniel, but he noticed something different about him. Daniel seemed scared and a little meaner than the last time they both met 20 years ago. Conner was worried that something had happened to his friend he left so long ago, and he thought maybe part of it was his fault. But what did he do? He didn't know yet.

Conner had just finished catching two decently sized salmon when he noticed Daniel was packing to go.

"Hey, wait!" Conner said.

"Come on," Daniel started. "We can't waste any more time. You have to be faster if we both are going to leave this forsaken wilderness."

"Listen, we should at least eat breakfast first," Conner said. "We have a long way yet to go. We need energy for the journey."

After roasting the fish above the campfire, the two ate hastily. Conner was a little annoyed that Daniel was in such a hurry, but he also found it kind of helpful.

"I have a map to one of the Protector's bases, and we should be there by late this evening if we stay focused," Conner said.

"Tomorrow!" Daniel yelled. "I would rather be at the Son's Castle instead of seeing these Protectors!"

"I understand," Conner said. "But we need these Protectors' help whether we want them or not! We'll never make it past Lucien without them."

"Fine," Daniel replied, annoyed.

Chapter 8

The Tiger

As they traveled to the bases of the Protectors, they came across a large hole in the path of the road. Daniel peered inside to find a rather large cavern. It appeared empty from what they could see.

Daniel climbed down into the space.

"Daniel! I don't think that's a good idea!" Conner advised.

"Come on you scaredy cat!" Daniel yelled back to his friend. "Let's go check this out!"

Conner obviously didn't think it was a good idea, but he didn't want to leave Daniel down there alone. After Conner's feet hit the ground in the space, suddenly and seemingly out of nowhere, a tiger leaped out of the shadows.

"I was afraid a lion would come out of this den, but this is pretty dangerous, too," Conner whispered, trying not to move.

"Pretty cool you mean, right?" Daniel disagreed.

The tiger pounced on Conner and pinned him to the ground with one of his massive paws!

"OK, I'm starting to see why you say this is dangerous," Daniel finally agreed.

Daniel tried to hit the tiger with his sword, but the majestic beast was too fast and leapt off of Conner. Conner was unable to get up as he was still trying to catch his breath after the weight of the beast was released from his back.

The tiger pushed Daniel to the ground like a bull. The tiger bared its teeth and was about to kill Daniel, but then a sparkling white human form came out of the den and pushed the tiger to the ground. The tiger whined as it got up and tried to attack, but the dazzlingly bright man pounced on the tiger with such great strength that the tiger immediately died.

The man looked at Conner and Daniel, but didn't kill them. Conner and Daniel looked at each other, but when they looked back to see the man, He was gone!

"Conner, are you OK?" Daniel asked.

"Yeah, I think so, but I feel like I was almost crushed," Conner answered.

Daniel searched around the cavern until he found a large enough stick that Conner could use as a cane of sorts. Conner didn't mind. For the rest of their lives, they would never forget the tiger and the man.

Chapter 9

The Protectors

After the incident with the tiger, the duo decided to get some rest in the den. Daniel was happy to have a nap after his disjointed sleep the night before. In the afternoon, they left the den and embarked on their journey, which wasn't as long as Daniel thought it would be.

"We should be there before sunset, so hopefully they will have some good food ready there," Conner replied as he was looking at the map.

Daniel wondered what the protectors would be like. Would they be as friendly as Conner made them sound or would they be enemies?

Before he knew it, the two of them saw in the distance what must be the base. Conner saw a sign that read: THE PROTECTORS' STATION #1. That meant they were at least 30 minutes away from the Protectors' camps.

"What's the plan?" Daniel asked Conner.

"We are going to ask for dinner, and hopefully they will say yes. Then we can discuss our desire to leave with them. Do you think that's a good plan?"

"I've heard better ones, but I can't think of a better plan," Daniel answered.

Soon, a big gate stood in front of them, and Conner knocked a special code that let the people inside know they meant no harm.

"How do you know that code?" Daniel wondered aloud. "You aren't a Protector, are you?"

"Actually, I am," Conner smiled, finally revealing his secret to Daniel. "That's why I have this black and blue cloak. Well, I am still training to become a Protector X, which is a leader rank. I am a Protector R. We need more Protectors that can help us on our journey."

They walked through the gateway, and many Protectors greeted them. One of them was the Protector Z, the leader of the base, and his name was Peter. Daniel learned that only 12 people held the rank of Protector Z.

"Conner, it's good to see you again!" Peter exclaimed. "And it seems you have a friend. Welcome to Talhum."

"Yes, and his name is Daniel," Conner replied. "We would like to have dinner with you and discuss something."

"Well, sure, I have time to eat with you and your friend," Peter answered. "There is some lamb being made with bread. Would you and your friend enjoy that?"

"Absolutely," Daniel said, as his stomach growled.

Chapter 10

Dinner With Peter

Peter led them into a huge building with a long table that had lamb and several loaves of bread that had been prepared for them. They all sat down for their dinner and conversation.

"What is it that you want to discuss with me?" Peter asked. "And why is it that you in particular came to this base?"

"We need you and some of the other Protectors' help so me and my friend, Daniel, can finally go home," Conner replied.

"I don't know if I can do that because we still need to stop Lucien and his army," Peter answered. "We really do want to help you get out of this mess, but there's really nothing we can do to help you and Daniel."

"Look," Conner started. "We can maybe help you by gathering all of the Protectors from every base and leading an attack on Lucien wherever he is. If we defeat him, then you can help us leave."

"That will never be enough, though, because in a prophecy it is said that only the Son can defeat

Lucien, but Lucien only goes for us," Peter said. "He knows he can't kill the Son, so he tempts us and kills every Protector and village he can!"

Silence lingered over the table as they all took a break from talking and ate some of their lamb and bread.

"Then why don't we just go to the Son's Castle?" Daniel asked before he could think long enough to stop himself. "Then we can just fight Lucien there and hopefully the Son joins in and helps."

Daniel had finally said something meaningful to their journey.

"We would need all of the Protectors in the Kingdom to make it to the Son's Castle," Peter said.

THUD. THUD. Loud sounds came from outside the building. Before they had time to figure out the source of the noises, fire began to engulf the building. Peter, Conner, and Daniel crouched under the table to protect themselves from the fire and formulate an escape plan.

Chapter 11

The Battle of Talhum

Fire was spreading across the room, and Daniel, Conner, and Peter didn't know what to do.

"What are we going to do, sir?" Conner asked Peter.

"Run as fast as you can towards the door so we can get out and figure out what is happening," Peter commanded.

Quickly they all ran from the fire towards the door, but Daniel tripped on one of the table's legs, and the fire was spreading around him.

"Help!" Daniel yelled to Peter and Conner.

Peter grabbed a pitcher of water and threw it to the ground, and it put out the fire around Daniel. Daniel got to his feet and ran out through the door.

Once outside the base, the three of them saw fire everywhere. Lucien's henchmen were wreaking havoc all around, and Lucien himself was floating above them in the air with his wings.

"Lucien," Peter said, angrily.

"We have to fight!" Conner shouted.

They all unsheathed their swords and held them at the ready, shouting orders to all the other Protectors.

"Ready your weapons for battle!" Peter commanded.

"What will be the use, Peter?" Lucien asked, wickedly. "Or should I use your old name?"

"I prefer my new name," Peter answered.

"You all have two choices," Lucien spat. "Either you join me, and you will all live. Or you could fight, and you will all die."

"I'd rather die than work for you because what you promise is the worst death!" Peter exclaimed. "Death in your land! Away from the one who made me and my friends! I don't want that!"

"Me, too! And Daniel!" Conner agreed.

Daniel started thinking. Which would be better? Life or death? Peter said that working with Lucien would lead to the worst death.

"What will it be?" Lucien asked, glaring directly at Daniel.

"I choose… Peter and Conner!" Daniel said.

"Well, enjoy death!" Lucien growled.

Lucien and his army charged towards the Protectors. Daniel fought with his sword as hard as he possibly could, but he still wasn't completely trained. However unsure he felt with the sword, he still killed five of Lucien's henchmen. Conner and Peter were in the hundreds.

Lucien's army boasted 50,000 troops. The Protectors had 30,000. Lucien went through most of the Protectors he faced easily, but when he saw Peter, ready to fight him, Lucien knew he was in for a fight.

Lucien flew towards Peter and swung his sword. Peter easily blocked it and threw his sword at Lucien, hitting him in the chest. Despite the blow, Lucien didn't seem like he was dying. Lucien pulled the sword out of his chest and flung it to the ground.

When Lucien was about to throw a strike at Peter, the shining man who killed the tiger came out of the forest and pounced on Lucien, nearly killing him. Peter was relieved at the sight of the shining man and fought more of Lucien's troops with renewed spirit.

The shining man ran back into the forest, and Lucien flew away, retreating to recover in his stronghold. Lucien's troops stayed in the fight.

Conner was ready to rest, but he had to keep fighting. He saw a bow on the ground and fired at some of the flying troops.

Daniel was captivated watching Conner and Peter fight and slay so many of Lucien's troops. Unaware of his surroundings, Daniel did not notice one of Lucien's firing an arrow at Daniel. The arrow landed right in Daniel's chest, instantly knocking him unconscious to the ground. Conner saw Daniel crumple to the ground.

"No!" Conner cried as he ran towards the almost

dead Daniel. "Peter! Help!"

Peter ran to Conner and lifted the unconscious Daniel on his back. Daniel was starting to wake up and noticed that it sounded like the man was coming out of the forest to attack again, and he was still covered in a shining light. He came back out of the forest and was staring at him. Daniel was confused at why the shining man was looking at him specifically. He was also kind of terrified.

Daniel was being carried towards a small camp that was simply called the "triage room" and was laid on a bed. Peter went back out of the camp to keep fighting the troops. Conner stayed in the room for a while so he could keep Daniel safe, but after a short time, he was drawn back out to keep fighting.

As Conner exited the camp, he was greeted by a punch straight in the face, and he face-planted on the ground. It was one of Lucien's troops. The demon soldier went into the triage room to find Daniel, who was still unconscious on the bed.

Conner raced to get back to his feet and landed an arrow in the troops heart and killed him. A horn blew, and Lucien's remaining troops began retreating.

Of all Lucien's troops that were killed, Peter took down the most, but he had arrows and wounds all over him and was led to the nursing room to get help.

Daniel woke up the next morning with no arrow in his chest. Instead, bandages were in place of it. He got up and went to go find Peter and Conner. He found them outside grieving near all of the Protectors who died the night before.

Chapter 12

The Loss

Two thousand Protectors died in the battle, and 15,000 were wounded, including Peter. One thousand of Lucien's troops were dead, and 13,000 were wounded.

Daniel saw a pile of Protectors who were waiting to be nursed back to health by the doctors in the triage room. The doctors at the base were incredibly skilled and could heal even the most severe wounds if treated quickly enough. Their skills and gifts had saved Daniel and were saving many others, too.

"What are we going to do now?" Daniel asked.

"What you suggested because it's the most logical solution," Peter answered.

"We will leave tomorrow and gather all of the Protectors, but we need to be careful," Conner said. "One of the Protectors Z is not as trustworthy as the others like Peter."

"Why?" Daniel asked.

"He has mentioned his doubts that it might be that Lucien will win," Peter answered.

"He also has a thing about money," Conner added.

"Can't blame him," Daniel said.

Conner rolled his eyes. Before he could respond to Daniel, an entry-level Protector entered and addressed Peter.

"Sir, one of our most important soldiers, Jacob, is missing," the young Protector said. "Some reports from our soldiers say one of Lucien's troops took him captive."

"The good thing is that we are going to the other Protector camps to negotiate with the other Protector Zs and then going to the Son's castle to fight the final battle!" Peter replied. "We will go find Jacob along the way, too."

Daniel, Conner, and Peter all packed essential items for the adventure. Daniel packed a sword, a shield, a bow and arrow, several loaves of bread, and a canteen full of water. After the trio had finished packing, they left the base to gather the other 11 Protector Zs, find their missing Protector, Jacob, and prepare for the final battle.

Chapter 13

The Adventure

Daniel wasn't expecting to have much fun on the journey to gather all the Protectors, and he was right. He found himself bored and decided to be annoying like he was with his "friends."

"So, are we there yet?" Daniel asked, like a child on a road trip.

"NO!" Peter and Conner replied in unison.

"So, why is this Protector guy, Jacob, so important?" Daniel asked.

"He is one of the most powerful, strong, and helpful Protectors we have at my base," Peter said. "But with him supposedly being captured, it brings suspicion."

"Remember, Peter," Conner started. "Jacob is a kind and respectable Protector, ready to do anything to help us win."

"One more question," Daniel wondered aloud. "Who do you and the other Protectors protect?"

"We protect the villages and cities around us," Peter answered.

Although Daniel said he only had one more question, he in fact, had more.

"How long is it going to take us to find Jacob?" Daniel complained.

"Boy, stop with these infernal questions, or we'll be forced to bound and gag you," Peter said.

Daniel made eye contact with Conner, shrugged his shoulders, and dropped his head.

"Where do you think Lucien's troops took Jacob?" Conner asked, getting questions in for Daniel.

"He is most likely at the abandoned base of the Destroyers," Peter said, giving Conner a slightly scolding look.

"Destroyers?" Daniel couldn't help but ask.

"That's the name given to Lucien's troops," Conner said. "We burned that base in the great Battle of Tears. We destroyed the base, but we lost 10,000 Protectors that day. The most we've ever lost in a single battle."

Daniel looked confused, but he was wary to ask another question. Peter took notice and began speaking as if he was able to read Daniel's mind.

"The Battle of Tears was a battle that defined a generation," Peter said. "It was a gruesome battle, and it came at a great cost. We lost so many Protectors that day that our villages were left vulnerable for a long time. Many tears were shed for years to come because many were without Protectors to keep them safe. It took us years to recapture our bases and build our troop count back up."

Daniel noticed that Conner's countenance had fallen at the mention of the Battle of Tears.

"Conner, you were there?" Daniel asked.

"Yes, and I am glad you weren't there because you would not have survived that day," Conner answered.

Peter simply shook his head in agreement. Daniel felt bad for not being like Conner and Peter. He wasn't strong and skilled in fighting like they were, and worst of all, he didn't have faith in the Son like them.

As they reached the top of a small hill, they could now see a large base wall through some of the trees in the valley below. It reminded Daniel of the wall around Peter's base, except for all the black scorch marks covering it. From the look of it, Daniel immediately knew it must be the abandoned Destroyer base.

Chapter 14

The Abandoned Base

"You keep saying the base is abandoned, but how do you know for sure?" Daniel asked.

"After the fires, it was left uninhabitable," Peter said. "But it's been years. Only one way to find out if it still is abandoned or not."

They found a door and entered because it was not locked or barricaded, as Peter anticipated. They walked through the ruins and wreckage of the base. Most of the walls were either destroyed by the fires or finished off by the elements in the years since.

"Man, this place is a dump," Daniel said. "It reminds me of a landfill. Good thing this place got destroyed! Even without burning it, it doesn't seem like it looked much better before this happened!"

Conner elbowed him in the chest, gently.

"Hey, man, you don't have to be so rude," Conner said.

"These monsters are your enemies," Daniel said. "What do you care what I say about them?"

"We can be better than that," Conner insisted.

Before Daniel could protest, they all heard a clatter of tools in the room ahead of them.

"Jacob!" Peter whispered excitedly.

"How could he possibly know it's him?" Daniel asked Conner.

Peter ran up to the door, but it was locked. He had to back up to gain momentum to kick it open. The three of them were surprised and shocked. In the room, bound to a chair, was their lost Protector, Jacob. But he wasn't alone. Lucien was standing right there next to the bound Jacob with a knife held up to his neck.

"Jacob! Are you all right!?" Peter exclaimed.

"Not at this particular moment," Jacob answered sadly.

"He will be even less fine in a moment," Lucien said menacingly. "I will put an end to his life unless he becomes a turncoat, joins me, and becomes one of my most valuable Destroyers in my army."

"Don't!" Peter cried.

"What do you want, Jacob?" Lucien asked. "Life or death?"

"I would rather die at your hands than join your army," Jacob answered bravely.

"If you join, you will have a family again!" Lucien tried to entice Jacob. Jacob had lost his family in the Battle of Tears.

"I already have a family!" Jacob declared as he

raised his arm, pointing to Peter, Conner, and Daniel. "This is my family, and I won't deny them even though I will die! If I join you, I am dead, but if I join the Son, I am alive! And you can't do anything but lie to try to take that away from me!"

Jacob's bravery shocked Daniel, but it greatly aggravated Lucien. Lucien took the knife away from his neck and plunged it into his chest, killing Jacob. Peter and Daniel were stunned, but Conner immediately pulled out a dagger and threw it at Lucien in a fit of rage.

Lucien caught the dagger by the blade and crushed it in his palm, turning it to dust. Conner started to charge towards Lucien, but Peter grabbed him firmly from behind and stopped him.

"Conner, you know we can't defeat him on our own," Peter urged him.

Lucien looked up at them, pulled the knife out of Jacob's chest and vanished before their eyes. Conner ran up to Jacob's body, fell at his feet and wept.

"I'm sorry, Conner," Peter said. "I know Jacob was like a brother to you. This is an unspeakable loss:"

The three of them carried Jacob's body out of the base and buried him in a nearby clearing. Exhausted physically and emotionally, the trio rested near the burial site.

Chapter 15

Meeting Philip

Daniel's mind was racing.

"If I join you, I am dead, but if I join the Son, I am alive."

What had Jacob meant with those words? How could he be alive if his choice would lead to death? And if the Son didn't save him, how could He be so good?

The morning following Jacob's death, the trio had pressed onward. They had been traveling for hours when Peter finally saw a Protector's base.

"This is Philip's base," Peter said. "Welcome to Betsada."

"What is this Philip guy like," Daniel asked Conner.

"I'm not sure," Conner said. "I've never met him. But Peter and Philip have known each other for ages."

Philip was kind and showed great hospitality to his guests. Over a meal, the trio caught Philip up on the events of the last few days.

"You want to go to the Son's castle?" Philip asked.

"Yes," Peter explained. "We need to lure Lucien's army to the castle, and hopefully the Son will come down and finally end this like the prophecy said."

"We can't go to the Son's castle," Philip replied.

"Why not!?" Daniel yelled, exasperated.

"There is a great chasm between where our land ends and his castle," Philip answered. "We will never be able to make up the gap."

"We have to try," Peter said. "We have no choice."

Philip paused in thought before responding.

"How many Protectors will we need?" he asked.

"Every single one," Peter said slowly.

Chapter 16

The Battle of Betsada

Peter, Conner and Daniel were still discussing the plan with Philip when the floor started to rumble. Daniel fell out of his seat.

"Daniel, are you OK?" Philip asked, concerned.

But Daniel didn't answer. He was unconscious.

"Daniel, wake up!" Conner yelled, worried for his friend.

"Don't worry," Peter said. "He is still breathing."

Peter was correct. Daniel wasn't dead, but Conner noticed that he had a small dart on his back.

"It must be some kind of tranquilizer," Conner said.

Suddenly, an eerie tune began to play in the distance. It sounded like it was coming from a horn. Philip knew the tune all too well.

"They're here," Philip said gravely.

Peter and Philip left the room urgently to gauge just how severe the fight would be. Conner was frozen for a moment. He felt terrible at the thought of leaving Daniel in the room alone, but he didn't know what else to do. He felt compelled to go and fight.

Conner gave one last look at Daniel, and then ran towards the door. Conner was immediately pushed aside as he stepped through the threshold. The assailant was one of Lucien's trusted troops, Arnold.

"Look, if you want to live, don't fight!" Arnold said menacingly.

"I don't give up!" Conner answered.

Conner tackled Arnold to the ground and knocked him out. He grabbed his bow and arrow and started to shoot down the flying troops.

Daniel slowly woke up and saw through sluggish, blurred eyes Lucien's troops around him. They tied him up, gagged him so he couldn't yell for help and carried him out of the base. Daniel was still too groggy to fight back.

Outside Peter was fighting one of the toughest of Lucien's troops. He was 7-foot-2, which was a terrifying height for Peter because that was about a foot taller than himself. Peter landed his dagger into the troop, but the giant appeared unharmed. The troop grabbed Peter forward, punched him in the face and knocked him out.

Conner noticed and shot an arrow at the troop and killed him. Then he saw a gagged Daniel being carried away by Lucien's troops.

"Peter, they captured Daniel!" Conner cried. Peter

came to, hurried to his feet and ran to stop them with Conner.

Daniel's vision was gradually restoring and getting clearer. He suddenly saw Lucien in front of him and felt like he was dead already.

"Daniel! It is so nice to see you again!" Lucien said.

Daniel was untied and ungagged by the troops so he could talk. Daniel was frightened. He wanted to run away into the forest, but he knew he couldn't get far.

"Again, I am going to give you two choices," Lucien said. "Come with me, and you will live. Refuse to join me, and you will be killed with this sword."

Lucien took a sword out and held it out.

"Choose!!!" Lucien yelled.

Peter and Conner caught up and saw what was going on, and they were furious. They knew what Lucien was doing.

"I choose…" Daniel struggled.

Conner was scared for him.

"I choose…" Daniel tried to answer.

Conner aimed his bow and shot an arrow at Lucien. The arrow bounced off him.

Lucien's eyes glowed with anger, and Daniel took advantage of the distraction to run away towards the forest. Lucien took flight to chase Daniel, and Conner and Peter followed.

Daniel ran for his life. He knew that if he wasn't fast enough, he would die or be forced with the choice again. He tripped on a branch, fell into a creek and was soaked! He hid behind a log in the creek. Lucien landed slowly and began lurking slowly across the path next to the creek. Daniel was terrified. Lucien's fangs were bared as he prowled slowly across the path. He could feel Lucien's anger radiating out of him. He knew Lucien wanted him dead.

After what felt like an eternity, Lucien launched himself into the air again and flew away. He had not seen Daniel hiding behind the log in the creek.

With Lucien gone, Daniel ran out of the forest and found a road. He followed it, hoping it would lead back to the base. Before long, he had a problem.

The road split into two paths, and Daniel had no idea which one to take. He moved towards the left path until he heard familiar voices.

Peter and Conner were running towards him. They wanted to help him, but Daniel stopped them.

"I am going to find a way to die," Daniel said.

"Daniel, no!" Peter yelled. "You don't want to do that."

"It's better than being stuck here forever!" Daniel argued. "What if dying here gets us back home? Back to the real world!"

Peter looked at Conner, concerned.

"Can Daniel and I have a quick word with each

other?" Conner asked.

Peter nodded and stepped back.

"Daniel, what's going on?" Conner asked. "You are a different person than I remember. What happened?"

"What do you mean I'm different?" Daniel asked.

"I mean that you're not as kind or patient as you used to be," Conner said. "And you don't listen."

"I lost…" Daniel struggled. "I lost my parents after you left. It's been hard without you all those years. I lost my friend first and then my parents. Conner, I don't believe what you believe anymore. I gave it up at my parent's funeral."

"Gave it up?" Conner asked. "You mean you gave up on God?"

"I lost everything!" Daniel said, agony in his voice. "And now this dream is killing me! I don't know where I am, but I will tell you one thing. I would rather die than stay here!"

"Daniel," Conner pleaded. "Once I nearly quit on everything I believed in, but I knew what I believe is true. Don't give up. Please!"

"I just don't know that I can believe again," Daniel replied. "And I can't stay here."

"Just promise me you'll keep going," Conner said. "We have each other again now. We can at least keep going for each other."

"Fine," Daniel said. "For each other."

Chapter 17

The Journey Continues

Daniel still wanted to run away, but he wanted to keep his promise to Conner.

"Promises shouldn't be broken," Daniel's mom would say, so Daniel made sure he wouldn't.

Conner was a little traumatized from what Daniel told him. Daniel gave up on his faith in God? That hurt Conner, but maybe the Son would help Daniel. Daniel's parents died. Conner never had to face a loss like that. A dead goldfish could hardly compare. Daniel was an orphan. Conner couldn't imagine how hard that was for him.

Conner did know what it was like to miss parents, though. He didn't know how long it had been since he had seen his parents. It felt like years… But Conner was confident he would see them again. Daniel did not have that hope. Especially now.

When they returned to Philip's base, the host was worried about the continued battles that kept popping up with Lucien.

"We will have to stop having these run-ins with

Lucien and his troops if we have any hope of gathering all the Protectors and making it to the Son's Castle any time in the next century," Philip said.

Daniel was too distracted to pay much attention to their plans. Ever since he arrived in this dream, something had been stirring within him. It was uncomfortable. It felt like he was being forced to face things he did not want to face.

There had been a time when Daniel sort of believed God exists, but after he lost Conner and then ultimately his parents, he had let go of any notion of God. Daniel was angry, and he couldn't let go of his anger. If he was honest with himself, he would admit that a small part of him did still believe God was real, and God was where he had been aiming all of his anger for many, many years. But Daniel was rarely honest with himself since his parents had died.

Jacob's last words still puzzled him. *"If I join you, I am dead, but if I join the Son, I am alive!"* If only Daniel had that faith.

"Come on, Daniel," Peter said, snapping Daniel out of his thoughts. "We have to go."

"Are the Protectors from this base going to follow us to the Castle of the Son?" Daniel asked as they departed the base.

"Yes," Peter said. "Philip and his protectors will travel with us now. We all have the same destination."

"Get ready for a long trip," Conner said.

Daniel was never a big fan of road trips, and he was suddenly aware of how hungry he was.

"I could sure go for a sausage and egg biscuit right about now," Daniel said. "I know that when I'm starving in the morning, a Chick-fil-A biscuit sure does me good."

"What is Chick-fil-A?" Peter asked. "And what are sausage and egg biscuits?"

"You know, sausage, it's a patty formed from meat from a pig," Daniel said.

"A pig!" Peter laughed. "No, sir, we eat mostly lamb around here."

Peter was beginning to enjoy the time he was spending with Daneil, but there was something missing from him. His faith. Peter understood. Daniel was alone with no family. Daniel wasn't given a choice. But ultimately, no one can choose or control what happens to the people they love.

"We ran out of the lamb, but we still have that amazing bread," Peter said.

Peter was still troubled by the fact that the Son might not even come to help if they somehow were able to complete their journey to his castle. Peter knew he couldn't force Him to help them in their most important battle yet. The prophecy from the Book of the Son stated the Son would come to help His people when the time was right. Is that time now?

Chapter 18

James

After already having visited two other Protector bases, Daniel could tell from a distance that the place they were approaching was another base. It was the simple structure that he had gotten used to in this world. It boasted several 100-foot-tall towers, and the closer you got to it, the more difficult it became to keep its entire width within view (there were at least 30,000 Protectors held within each base with iron and stone walls to protect them). This was James' base.

Peter knocked on the main entrance door. He knocked seven times, which was a standard way of knowing it was another Protector who was knocking on your door. A Protector opened the door and welcomed them in and took them to James, who was excited to see them, especially Peter.

"Peter!" James exclaimed. "It's been so long!"

Peter hugged his good friend in equal happiness. Daniel wished he had a lot of friends like that, but he didn't. It wasn't for a lack of trying. Daniel knew he had many people in his life who were willing to be a friend to him, but it was himself that kept that from happening. He would keep that in mind when he got back home. If he ever did get home…

As they had approached the base, Conner at first thought it was just like any other base based on the outside, but boy was he wrong. On the inside of the base, it was filled with houses and people and markets for food and everyday necessities. Conner didn't understand why, but there was a whole village inside the Protector base.

"James, why is there a village in this base?" Conner asked.

James looked back at him gravely. His whole demeanor changed at the question. Peter made a sad expression as well.

"This used to just be a village, not a Protector base," Peter explained. "It used to be a city actually filled with markets and pubs, restaurants, homes, and theaters to go watch plays. It was even the town that me and James and all of the Protector Zs were born and raised. It was where me and the others met the Son. He wasn't born here because He always existed with His Father."

"Well, what happened?" Daniel wondered. "Why is it now a mix of a base and a village?"

"After the Son returned to His castle, Lucien decided it was time to strike," Peter said. "He destroyed the village and burned the houses and killed most of the citizens here. He even broke my left arm."

Peter raised his arm to reveal a large scar between his wrist and elbow.

"Our parents were killed," Peter said solemnly. "Our friends were killed. That's how the Protectors were born. We built this base first with bricks and mortar. Then eventually we were able to add iron around the village, and James became the leader of this base. Me and the other Protector Zs started their own bases. I eventually started a family and brought them to my base."

Daniel didn't understand.

"Why didn't the Son come to help?" Daniel asked. "Didn't He know you?"

"He does know us," Peter answered. "In fact, He knows everyone who was ever born, but He said that we would face persecution for what we believe… for following Him. Belief doesn't stop the troubles and horrors of this world. Only He can do that. He said He would return to finally end this and Lucien's schemes, but we don't know when that will happen. Not even He knows the hour. Only the Father knows that. But the Son will come someday. We believe that, and we stand guard for His return."

"That honestly sounds unfair, doesn't it?" Daniel accused.

"Try to imagine you were a perfect being who had

a Father who created everything and was perfect as well," Peter said. "Who do you think would be better equipped to decide what is fair? The creator or the creation?"

Daniel turned away. He understood what Peter was trying to say, but he still couldn't completely believe it.

Seriously, how could I believe in all of this crazy stuff, he thought. *This is just a dream. I will wake up soon and come back to my senses.*

As soon as he thought it, he began to doubt even those thoughts. What if he never woke up? Would he ever return home? Maybe this really is not a dream? All of these thoughts puzzled and terrified Daniel for the rest of the day.

One thought terrified him the most. What if… the Son doesn't send me home? What if… He doesn't like me enough because of what I believe? Daniel had a feeling he might never leave.

Chapter 19

The Mission in Shalom

James was immediately onboard with the trio's plan, but he needed help with his own mission first. The mission was to ambush one of Lucien's secret bases. Its location made it particularly valuable to Lucien. Daniel was annoyed that James had a request of his own because it made the possibility of going home take even longer.

James told them about a large city a few hours away called Shalom. It was a city with nearly a million people. The thought of that many people made Conner feel claustrophobic.

"Why do you want us to go on this mission?" Daniel complained. "Why can't you send others to do it?"

James was patient with him.

"Daniel, I understand that you need to go home," James said calmly. "But we need all of the help we can get with this mission, and I will be there, too, to do this. This base is embedded right in the middle of a huge city. If we can force them out, we can keep a lot of people in the city safe."

Daniel was getting tired of all of the fighting. Sure, Peter, Philip, James, and Conner were great warriors, but Daniel wasn't. He was not like them. But he had no sway in this decision. The others were all convinced. Shalom was a huge city with large walls to surround it. It was a city that was guarded by Protectors, but Lucien's troops were rumored to be hiding there. James had a soldier who believed he had uncovered the secret location of Lucien's new base within the city. The goal was to crush Lucien's presence in the city before it gained more of a foothold.

"Who told you that Lucien's troops were hiding here?" Conner asked James when they entered Shalom.

"We've always had Protectors here to keep the city safe," James said. "I have had my own spies embedded here from time to time to keep an eye out for any emerging threats. One of my spies said he saw Lucien's sign here. This man is among some of my most trusted spies."

Daniel had expected this town to be more modern than what he had previously seen in this world given the size, but it wasn't. There were markets, little houses, and schools for children. There were also wells for water, but Daniel felt suspicious about them. One of them had a strange sign on it. Two swords clashing with each other with writing on the bottom that said: "Join us, and you will be free to do whatever you want. Refuse to join us, and you will die."

"Peter, that sign reads familiar," Daniel pointed.

Peter looked at that sign and walked over to the well. Another sign was hanging and read: "NO WATER IN THIS WELL!"

Daniel walked over to the well and leaned over to look in. When he placed both hands on the well to support himself as he looked down into it, the stones beneath his hands immediately gave way. Daniel fell forward into the well.

"DANIEL!" Conner yelled, concerned for his friend.

Conner leaped to the well and looked down to find his friend. To his great relief, Daniel was a few feet down inside the well, tightly gripping a ladder on one wall that extended down further into the well.

"Daniel, are you OK!?" Conner yelled.

"Yeah, I think so," Daniel responded.

James quickly bought torches from one of the markets. He lit one and dropped it into the well. It fell past Daniel and illuminated the well as it fell to the bottom.

"Daniel, it looks like you'll be leading us to the bottom as you have the head start," James said with a smile.

They all climbed down the ladder, and they eventually found themselves in a dimly lit room. It was hard to tell how big it was, as the only light was coming from the single torch James had dropped. James handed out the other torches, and they lit them one by one. With each light, the room began to come more into focus.

They all scoured around the room to investigate. Daniel watched a lot of movies like this. The protagonist finds a secret room and discovers the hidden treasure. It gave him a tinge of excitement. Daniel looked everywhere he could, but he didn't see anything of value. The room seemed entirely empty, but Daniel noticed an outline on a nearby wall.

"Hey, I think there's a door right here, see," Daniel pointed out.

Peter saw the outline, too. "Yeah, it is! Great job Daniel."

For the first time since arriving in this world, Daniel felt valued. They walked up to the door and opened it and were shocked at what they found inside. The room was filled with drawings of what Daniel recognized to be some of the Protectors, including Jacob. He guessed many of the other faces must also be Protectors. Daniel felt terrified, but didn't know exactly why. It felt like some evil plan was in progress, and the people in these drawings were being targeted.

"These seem to be some of Lucien's most wanted Protectors," Philip said. He saw that some of the drawings of the Protectors had markings scratched over their faces, specifically Jacob.

"Some of these are marked out," Philip said. "I guess these are the Protectors that they have killed."

Daniel's eyes darted quickly over all the faces. There were so many, and it was overwhelming to see how many had been marked out. As he continued to search the drawings, he was stunned by two of them hanging alone on one wall, as if they had been specifically singled out. One was Conner, and the other one was himself.

Daniel felt a rush of fear as any doubt that he was in danger had quickly been erased by finding these drawings.

Chapter 20

The Escape

As the fear continued to rise in Daniel, he heard footsteps beginning to echo back from near the well. They were no longer alone. He heard an evil chuckle he knew all too well. It was Lucien, and it sounded like a few soldiers were with him.

Daniel's heart was beating way too fast. His breathing quickened, too.

Conner noticed. "Daniel, are you OK?"

"Lucien's here," Daniel managed to whisper.

Conner could hear the footsteps now, too. He quietly closed the door to the room with the drawings, hoping it would give them time to find places to hide within the room. Lucien was now in the larger room off the room with the drawings.

"Where are they?" Lucien asked one of his soldiers, aggravated.

"They must be in there, sir," came the response.

Daniel, Conner, James, Philip and Peter quickly put out their torches and hid behind the many tables and shelves within the room.

The door creaked open.

Lucien stepped into the room with two soldiers trailing him. Each soldier held a torch.

"Before I deal with you, Daniel, and your pitiful lot," Lucien sneered. "I do have some work to tend to first."

Daniel was somehow met with even more fear as it was clear Lucien knew they were hiding in the room, but he was simultaneously relieved that all of his friends were hiding with him.

Lucien walked up to a particular desk, grabbed a drawing and pulled out a red ink pen.

"Leave your hiding spots," Lucien said calmly. "You're trapped in this room, so you might as well show yourself."

They all left their hiding spots. James reignited his torch to draw attention to himself.

"Let's play!" Lucien said viciously. He raised his sword.

Daniel and the others all unsheathed their swords, too. James leapt forward towards Lucien, the flame flickering from his torch drawing all eyes towards him. Peter also lunged from the opposite side of the room.

Lucien blocked James' strike and pushed him to the ground, but as his attention was focused on James, he did not have time to counter Peter. Peter shoved Lucien back into his soldiers, and they all collapsed past the door, giving an escape path for Daniel and the others.

James had dropped his torch when he hit the floor after Lucien's push. The torch had landed on one of tables covered with drawings and immediately caught fire. The fire spread quickly.

Conner ran to help James up, and Philip and Daniel ran towards Peter. Surprisingly quickly, all five were back on their feet and sprinting past the fire and smoke towards the well.

Lucien and his soldiers recovered and chased them in fury. Daniel was the last to climb up the ladder. The other four had already cleared the ladder before Daniel reached the top.

"DANIEL!!" Lucien screamed from the bottom of the well.

Daniel couldn't stop himself from looking back down. Lucien stood near the bottom of the ladder and raised his arms out to his sides. He was suddenly surrounded by swirling smoke and fire, as if all the fire and smoke caused by James' dropped torch was being absorbed into his body. Once all of the smoke and fire had been absorbed, he raised his arms up pointing towards Daniel. A great explosion erupted from his hands and exploded up through the well.

Daniel cleared the ladder just as the explosion escaped the well. The force of the explosion pushed

Daniel to the ground and knocked him unconscious.

Chapter 21

The Nightmare

"Where am I?" Daniel asked himself, confused.

Daniel was not with his friends.

"Guys? Where are you!?" Daniel cried out.

Daniel noticed he was at a school. He was walking around a hallway and right next to the kids' lockers, he noticed a familiar room. It was a schoolroom he attended when he was a child. Then he saw people whom he recognized. His old schoolteachers were walking down the hall in a hurry.

"Hey!" Daniel stopped them to talk.

"Who are you?" one of the teachers demanded. "You don't work here."

"Don't you remember me?" Daniel asked. "It's me, Daniel King!"

"That is an appalling thing to say," the teacher responded. "Especially on the day of his funeral. Don't make me get the principal or call security."

"Don't, please, I'm sorry," Daniel sputtered out. "Wait, my funeral? I'm not dead."

One of the teachers out of Daniel's sight called the

police, and they were on their way.

"No," Daniel said in agony. He ran from the teachers to find the nearest exit. He could hear sirens getting closer outside. He looked out of a window and saw it was the police. He found a door and ran to a bike rental and noticed he had his wallet with him, so he paid for it and started pedaling.

The police started to catch up with him, but Daniel saw his church. It wasn't the church he attended as a child with his parents, but rather it was the one he went to as an adult. The one he attended so he could torment his "friends." He got off his bike and entered the church to hide.

When he entered the sanctuary, he saw a funeral service was in progress. Three coffins were positioned near the altar. A large photo was displayed on a stand beside each coffin. Daniel stared at the photos, and the faces of his mother, father and himself started back at him. This was his parents' funeral. But it was also his funeral, too.

Daniel saw his "friends" from adulthood around his coffin, and they looked very sad.

"How did he die?" Daniel asked.

"He died in his sleep," Richard answered.

"Was he your friend?" Daniel asked.

"Yes, he was, despite himself and even though he was different," Richard said. "He didn't believe what we believed, and he even tried to disrespect it, but we wanted to be a good friend to him and maybe help him. But now he's gone. We prayed for him often, but we don't know if our prayers were answered with a yes."

Suddenly, the police stormed in and saw Daniel. Daniel ran from the policemen who were trying to catch him. He ran out of a side exit of the church and ran toward a bridge across the street. As he reached the middle of the bridge, two police cars raced in and blocked the path ahead, and the path behind him was now covered by the police who were pursuing him on foot.

Daniel was so frightened that he lost track of his surroundings as he backed up to the bridge's railing. He stumbled backwards onto the railing with too much speed fell over the side of the bridge.

"Ahhhhhh!!" Daniel yelled as he regained consciousness.

"Are you OK?" Conner asked the scared Daniel.

"Yeah, I think so," Daniel answered. He looked around him. It appeared they were on the outskirts of Shalom.

Chapter 22

The Final Base

Daniel was still reeling from his nightmare the next day, but he and the others had to continue on with the journey. The one positive from the mission in Shalom was that Lucien's secret base had been destroyed, and James was now ready and willing to lend his Protectors to the cause.

Daniel, Conner, Peter, Philip, and James left the James' base to finish meeting the other Protector Zs and pressing on to the Son's Castle. They trekked on to Matthew's base, then to Andrews' base, then to Thomas' base, John's base and more. Daniel got tired of all of the meetings with all of these Protector Zs. He found them tedious and boring, but he knew it was his only hope of escaping this world. Conner didn't mind the meetings. He was also excited for the glimmer of hope of returning home, and he wasn't one for wasting time.

The Protector meetings were important because they debated how they would fight Lucien's troops. Daniel didn't know for sure if Lucien was even alive after what happened to him in Shalom. How could anything survive that kind of explosion? But Peter, Conner, and the others disagreed. They knew that he couldn't be killed by them. They could resist his lies, but they couldn't kill him alone. Only the Son could.

Giving Daniel's argument (that Lucien was dead) some credibility was the fact that Lucien had not been encountered in the weeks after the mission and explosion in Shalom. The others had their own evidence, too.

"We know he isn't dead because we sent soldiers out to uncover more of his bases, and they haven't come back," John said. "We have this note from Lucien himself."

John handed Daniel the note, and Daniel read it aloud: "I have taken your friends when they came to spy on me, and my men and I have kept them imprisoned. I will come and visit you soon."

Daniel didn't buy it. "This isn't proof it is actually from Lucien. It could just be some tactic from his remaining soldiers to keep us afraid and inactive."

"If our Protectors really are being held, we have to try to save them!" Conner said.

"I'm not sure of how best to proceed," Peter didn't exactly agree. "The whole thing could possibly be a trap. I think we still need to visit the last lead Protector, Judas."

"What if we split up into teams," Conner said.

"Me and a few of the Protectors go search and save the captured soldiers while you, Daniel, and the others go meet Judas. I don't leave friends behind. Please."

Conner was a loyal, honest friend. He couldn't stand the thought of leaving behind other Protectors in need. Peter and Daniel both knew that, but they also knew that it was too risky. But before they could voice their concerns again, Conner interjected first.

"I will be back tomorrow, with our lost friends," Conner said.

"Conner, don't!" Daniel ordered.

"I have to go," Conner said. "I will come back, and if I don't, I know you guys will do your best to do what I am doing right now: serving my friends."

Daniel was afraid to lose Conner after being reunited with him after all these years, but he knew there was no changing his mind. Daniel was afraid because he still wasn't the best at fighting or defending his friends. He wasn't a warrior like Conner, but he knew he had to try his best.

Conner left the base with a few loyal Protectors and set off to track their lost comrades. Peter led the other Protectors and Daniel to Judas' base, which was less than a day's journey away in the region of Falhone. When they arrived, they were greeted by two Protectors, and they were led through the camps and rooms till finally they entered Judas' chamber.

"Sir, we have guests," one of the soldiers informed the host. "They are good friends of yours."

Judas immediately recognized Peter, James, John, Andrew, and the others. This excited him.

"Greetings, friends!" Judas said with a sly smile. "It's so exciting to see you all. It's nice to see most of my friends... and to meet new ones."

Judas' eyes rested upon Daniel.

"The only Protector Z I can't see is Philip," Judas said. "Where did he go?"

"He went with Conner on a separate mission," Peter answered.

"And what mission would that be?" Judas wondered.

"It's a search and rescue," Daniel said. "Conner believes that we have some soldiers who have been captured by Lucien. He believes Lucien is still alive. Some of us are unsure."

Judas' face went pale.

"Lucien," Judas whispered. "I don't think your friends should have messed with him. Those hostages are definitely dead. He set Conner up. He wants him dead, too!"

"You speak as if you know this as fact!" Daniel accused.

"I know what he does," Judas answered. "It would make the most sense for him to do this."

Daniel gave Peter a skeptical look.

"You must be starving!" Judas changed the subject.

Peter wanted to refuse, but he decided to play along for now. They all walked to the dining room and took a seat for dinner. The meals were set on the table in only a matter of minutes.

"We have to tell you something, Judas," Peter started. "We are going to fight Lucien at the Son's Castle, and hopefully the Son will come and stop him. Remember the prophecy that said that the final battle will happen at the Son's Castle?"

Judas didn't seem too happy.

"Do you need me for this?" Judas asked.

"Yes," Peter answered. "We need all 12 of the Protector Zs."

"I'm afraid I am unable to honor this request!" Judas said emphatically.

"Why do you not want to do this?" Peter asked.

"Lucien's going to win," Judas announced.

"No, he is not!" James screamed.

"And why exactly do you think Lucien's going to win?" Peter asked. "You know the prophecy. You walked with the Son. How could you believe Lucien could win?"

"He assured me he would," Judas answered coldly.

"You work for him!?" Daniel exclaimed.

"Yes, in fact I do," Judas spat, remaining in his seat at the head of the table.

Peter unsheathed his sword and held it out.

"Lucien won't win!" Peter said.

"Well, you can tell him that yourself," Judas replied as Lucien appeared in the air above the table.

"Judas is right," Lucien responded. "I will win this battle and this war. In fact, this is the final battle for all of you. Enjoy it!"

"You are wrong!" James yelled in anger.

Judas' Protectors began streaming into the great dining hall.

"Does it disappoint you to realize just how alone you truly are," sneered Lucien.

Meanwhile, Conner and Philip's search had led them to the region of Aemon, a territory controlled by Lucien. After hours of searching, the troupe discovered a stronghold that looked promising. Surprisingly, it appeared abandoned at the moment. The inside of the small base was dark and barren. Near the back, a door had a small glimmer of light surrounding its four edges. It was the only source of light in the whole place. Conner and Philip tiptoed to the door and slowly pushed it open.

"It can't be," Conner gasped when they saw what was behind the door.

Chapter 23

The Battle of Falhone

Daniel and the Protectors got in their fighting stances with their swords, and Peter was the first one to attack. Peter ran towards Lucien. Daniel faced Judas.

Conner couldn't believe his eyes! All of the Protectors that they had been searching for were all on the floor, dead.

"Lucien wanted us to come here," Philip said. "He's trying to split us up to make it easier to kill us."

"But how!?" Conner screamed. "No one is here but us!"

Suddenly, they heard voices from the other rooms. They were not alone after all. The voices became louder but weren't recognizable. The voices began to intensify all around them before suddenly going dead silent. Then out of nowhere, one of Lucien's troops jumped out of the shadows and wounded one of Philip's Protectors with his sword.

The battle was tragic. Peter fought with all his

might and strength, but it was no use. Lucien was stronger. He kicked Peter in the face and knocked him to the floor.

"Easy and pathetic," Lucien sneered. "If only he joined me. He would become more powerful than the others."

Peter rose and, enraged, threw all of his strength at Lucien. But the demon king countered again.

Daniel wasn't so lucky either. Judas wasn't stronger than him, but he was so slippery. He moved like a snake, making it near impossible to strike him with any accuracy. Trying to follow Judas' movements was dizzying. Judas punched Daniel in the stomach and knocked him over.

"Lucien was right," one of Lucien's troops said. "I didn't think you would be dumb enough to split up, but he knew you better than you knew yourselves, and you were dumb enough to come here to save your dead friends."

"After we're done with you, we'll be reunited with our friends soon enough," Conner said.

"Poor fool," another of Lucien's troops chimed in. "Lucien and Judas will have killed your friends by now."

"Judas… is working with Lucien?" Conner asked horrified.

Evil smiles began to spread across all of Lucien's

troops, and more and more seemed to be filing into the building. Conner, Philip and their Protectors were clearly outnumbered.

Conner threw his sword at the lead soldier, but just missed him. Lucien's soldier countered with a punch in the face, knocking Conner down to the dirt floor, unconscious. Philip stabbed the troop with his sword, mortally wounding him, but another soldier knocked him out with the handle of his sword.

James plowed through nearly every one of Lucien's troops and Judas' Protectors that he faced until he had made his way closer to Lucien and Peter. He noticed that Peter was unconscious before Lucien, and the demon king was about to strike the killing blow. James ran towards Lucien and leaped with his sword to stop Lucien's death blow. Lucien paused his motion and grabbed James' arm and threw him backward to the dinner table. Peter revived and took the fight back to Lucien.

James saw Daniel slumped to the floor in need while fighting Judas and ran right as Judas was going to strike Daniel with his sword. James blocked the attack and pushed Judas back.

"Why did you join him?" James demanded of Judas.

"I would have lost if I hadn't joined him," Judas answered.

"But you betrayed us, your friends," James cried in agony. "For what? Money!?"

"Survival," Judas replied cruelly as he threw a strike at James.

"You are a traitor!" James exclaimed as he dodged the attack.

Daniel got back up and punched Judas in the face.

"Ow!" Daniel yelled. "I thought that would hurt you, not me! I never knew it hurts so much to punch someone in the face."

The punch had stunned Judas, and before he collected himself, James threw another heavy punch to Judas' jaw. Judas fell down, unconscious.

"Fist bump!" Daniel said, holding out his fist to James. But James stared blankly, then walked away and cried alone. Daniel followed because he didn't understand.

"What's wrong?" Daniel asked.

"Judas was once my friend," James said. "It pains me that now he is my enemy. How would you feel if your friend betrayed you?"

Daniel thought of Conner, and he immediately understood how painful that would be.

"But come on, the fight's not done yet," Daniel urged James.

They joined Peter back in the dining hall, and the three of them stood together to face Lucien.

"Even with all three of you, are no match for the

dark side," Lucien laughed darkly.

"Hey, that's a Star Wars reference!" Daniel yelled. He was a huge Star Wars fan.

For the first time, Lucien looked confused. James and Peter also had no idea what Daniel was talking about. Daniel shrugged his shoulders and lunged forward with his sword towards Lucien. The demon easily avoided the attack and knocked Daniel to the ground.

One by one, James, Peter, and even John, mounted an attack on Lucien, and not a single one could manage to land a blow. It was futile.

"Retreat!" Peter ordered. No one disagreed with that order. All of Protector Zs, Daniel, and the remaining Protectors ran away from the base to stay alive.

Lucien held off his soldiers and let the Protectors flee. He had accomplished his goal of further reducing the Protectors' numbers. He had another place to be.

Chapter 24

End of the Line

As Conner regained consciousness, he could barely feel his face. In fact, after being out for hours, he couldn't really feel anything.

"Did you enjoy being so hopelessly outnumbered?" one of Lucien's troops taunted Conner.

Conner's vision finally started to lock back in. He tried to move his hands, but he quickly realized they were tied to the arms of a chair he was sitting in. He looked to his right and found Philip was next to him, also bound to a chair. Philip's eyes were fixed dead ahead on someone. Conner turned to see Lucien standing before them.

"What do you need from us?" Philip asked.

"What makes you think I need something from someone as meaningless as you two?" Lucien asked.

"Easy," Philip said. "The fact that we are still alive tells me you need something from us."

"I require information on what your friends are planning," Lucien said. "That's all."

"Like we would ever tell you, you monster!" Conner exclaimed.

"I have already killed the other Protectors who came with you, so only you and Philip remain," Lucien said. "But I have no intention of ending you yet. I have been and am continuing to be merciful to you. Honor my mercy by telling me what your plan is."

"Merciful," Conner yelled out in laughter. "You are not merciful. You are anything but merciful or good or just. You are the opposite of all of those things."

"Listen, I already know that you are planning to gather all the Protectors at the Son's Castle," Lucien said. "But I am trying to make sense of this lunacy. Even I know you can't just put the Son in a box. It's not like He's going to just say, 'They came to my castle, so I must help them.' He's not a genie obeying your every wish."

Philip began laughing. He laughed so much that he started wheezing and was out of breath.

"What's so funny, fool?" Lucien demanded.

"You just don't understand anything about the Son or why we believe in and follow Him," Philip said after catching his breath. "We have been praying to Him and have been asking Him to help us when we go there. He is just and mighty to save. The prophecy tells us He will return to save us. But maybe you're right. Maybe He won't this time. Even if He won't, we will still go and call on His name and worship Him. We trust that his rescue will be right on time, whether it is now or a thousand generations from now. You'll never understand because you never trusted Him. You only trust yourself."

Lucien smiled.

"Fine," he said. "I will take you to the Son's Castle myself. I want you to be there so I can see the hope drain from your souls when you realize he is not coming to rescue you. I want you to be there alongside your other Protectors, so you can all despair and die together. Perhaps I will give you one last chance to place your trust in me in the shadow of the Son's Castle."

Lucien walked to a table, scribbled a note on parchment, and gave it to one of his soldiers.

"Deliver that to John's base in Vanhorn," Lucien said. "It informs your friends that your entire party, including yourselves, have been killed at my hands, and that I will see them outside the Son's Castle."

Philip began laughing again.

"Of course," he said. "Lies are all you have. You lie to make us doubt what the Son will do. It's your only strategy."

Chapter 25

Faith

When Peter read Lucien's letter aloud to all of the others, Daniel was crushed. He lost his parents, lost his home, and now he completely lost his best friend, again.

Peter smiled.

"Conner and Philip live!" Peter rejoiced.

All the other Protectors began celebrating. Daniel was beyond confused.

"How could you possibly know that?" Daniel questioned. "Lucien is telling us they are dead!"

"When you believe the Son, you believe the truth," Peter said. "Lucien is the Anti-Son, which means he is the King of Lies, and truth cannot come from lies."

Daniel wanted to feel hope at Peter's declaration, but he still found himself feeling hopeless and downtrodden.

Peter noticed the sadness remaining on Daniel's face and knelt down close to him as the other continued to celebrate.

"What is it, son?" Peter asked.

"I am not a warrior," Daniel said. "I'm no leader. I

am nothing like you all. You guys are all strong and brave, but I'm not."

"What's holding you back?" Peter asked. "Being brave is not some innate ability. It's a choice. Like faith."

All at once, everything Daniel had been pushing back and trying to avoid facing rushed to the surface.

"I have no one," Daniel sobbed. "No one to protect me. I lost my parents when I was 8! I have no one who cares for me or loves me like a son! I missed out on lots of things in life because of that, and now I can't be like you. You guys do have people who support you. People you can trust. At least for a little longer I had Conner do that for me, but now he is gone! I know you think he is alive, but he's not. He's not because no one I love makes it. They all leave or are taken away. I am alone, and do you know who's fault that is? God! He is the reason I am alone."

Daniel dropped his head. When he looked back up, he expected to see disgust in Peter's face. Instead, he saw compassion.

"Daniel, you are not alone," Peter said. "We understand your pain. I lost my father at a young age."

"I lost a child just a few years ago," John said, joining them.

"I lost friends and family when Lucien attacked my village," James said.

"Is this supposed to make me feel better?" Daniel asked.

"That's not what we are trying to do," Peter said. "We want to tell you that we understand. Losing important people is a part of life. But the reason we haven't blamed the Father and the Son is because the Son told us that bad things will happen, and we will face heartache in this world. But He told us that it will be fixed in the end. You may have lost your parents Daniel, but you shouldn't give up on the Son and the Father. Daniel, you don't have to be a warrior like us, you just need to put your faith in the Son and Father like us."

Daniel, while feeling unburdened by finally saying all these things out loud, remained uncertain.

"Daniel, you have us," Peter said. "We support you and care about you. We are your friends. You might not feel it yet, but you are loved, not just by us, but also by the Son. We love because the Son first loved us. If Conner is truly dead like you believe, he would have wanted you to know that truth. But I believe he is still out there waiting to join us again."

Daniel didn't know what to say, so he just walked away in deep sadness and left the room to be alone.

All the remaining Protectors prepared to depart for the Castle of the Son the next morning. Before they left, Peter gathered them all for final words of encouragement.

"I won't keep anything from you," Peter said. "We embark to the Son's Castle to face the biggest battle of our lives! Death faces us all. I want you all to know that you are all loved. We are all friends and family under the Son. I do believe that the Son will fulfill the prophecy now. He is more than able to deliver us, and He will deliver us from Lucien's hand. But even if He does not, we will not bow a knee to Lucien. It has been an honor working and serving with you. Now, let's go fight the good fight!"

Chapter 26

Doubting Daniel

Daniel had lost track of how long he had been in the dream. A dream. That's what he was told he was experiencing. Or was it? He couldn't tell anymore. Had it been days? Months? Years? Conner had told him that you lose track of time when you're here.

All these questions and more were rattling around in Daniel's brain during the Protectors' advancement to the Son's Castle. But the biggest question that troubled Daniel the most…

Will I get home?

What if the Son doesn't want to send me home?

What if the Son doesn't exist?

If He doesn't exist… I won't go home!

Even Lucien seems to believe the Son exists… So, He has to exist!

"Hey, how are you holding up?" Peter asked him as they were taking a lunch break on the final day of their journey. "It seems like you're lost in conversation with yourself."

"I'm just worried about going to the Son's Castle,"

Daniel said. "What if the Son doesn't actually exist?"

"I promise you that He does exist," Peter said.

"That's easy for you to say," Daniel scoffed. "You claim to have known him face to face from long ago."

"Ah, yes, I've heard this complaint before," Peter said. "People have chastised us original Protectors for years, saying it's not fair for us to ask others to believe because it was easier for us because we saw what He did with our own eyes. You know, even being with Him for those years and serving with Him… Seeing Him minister to so many lost and hurting people… We saw Him do the miraculous every day. But even seeing it up close, it was always so hard for us to understand. His mission was so far beyond what we could comprehend. You know, even He had something to say about this once. He knew people would make this argument."

"Oh, yeah, what did he say about it?" Daniel asked.

"You should ask Thomas about it sometime," Peter said. "I don't want to speak for him, but the heart of it was something like this: 'Because you have seen me, you have believed. Blessed are those who have not seen me yet have believed.'"

Daniel nodded and wiped a tear from his cheek.

After a satisfying lunch, they left the Great Fields of Takiro for the two-hour remainder of their trek to the Great Twin Peaks of Takiro where the even greater Castle of the Son rests above the valley. There they would take part in the biggest battle of their lives.

Chapter 27

The Valley

Daniel couldn't believe his eyes. They were so close to the Son's castle! The castle looked beautiful unlike anything Daniel had ever seen. It just seemed to radiate strength and confidence.

But, as they had discussed before, there was one big problem. There was no way to actually get to the Castle. As the Protectors descended one of the Great Twin Peaks of Takiro to get down into the valley below the Castle, it became even more apparent that there was no way to reach it as it defied all natural law by hovering hundreds of feet above the valley.

"What now?" Daniel asked Peter and the Protector Zs.

"We will do as David and many of our other ancestors before us have done," Peter said. "We will for our Lord, who will answer."

For the first time in as long as Daniel could remember, he felt surprised at himself. A smile crept along his face.

"What's that smile about?" Peter asked, starting to

smile, too.

"This is just not how I thought I would feel," Daniel said.

"And how do you feel?" Peter asked.

"I feel… peace," Daniel said.

The Protectors set camp in the valley in the shadow of the Son's Castle and prepared themselves for battle.

On the other Great Twin Peak of Takiro, Lucien and his army prepared to descend into the valley to end the Protectors once and for all. First, Lucien had one last loose end to tie.

Two soldiers brought Judas to Lucien on the outskirts of the army.

"You wanted to see me?" Judas asked.

"Yes, here's the 30 pieces of Takiran silver you had requested as payment for betraying your precious Protectors," Lucien said, dropping a pouch of coins on the ground before him.

"Thank you, my Master," Judas said as he picked up the pouch. "Is there anything else?"

"As a matter of fact, I need you to run along ahead of us and join your precious Protectors down in the valley," Lucien said coldly.

"I don't understand," Judas said.

"I can't trust having a traitor in my midst at such a crucial juncture," Lucien said. "So go join those fools in the valley and await your incoming demise."

"I… I can't go back to them," Judas stammered. "I could never face them after what I've done. How could I?"

"Such is a traitor's dilemma," Lucien spoke smoothly. "But you are no longer welcome in my presence. Either face those you have hurt beyond repair, and you will surely be killed at their hands, or take matters into your own hands."

Lucien threw a rope down at Judas' feet.

"The decision is yours," Lucien said.

Judas, seized with remorse and unable to face his former Protectors, bent down and grabbed the rope.

Chapter 28

The Battle of the Valley

Daniel awoke suddenly the next morning to a loud, piercing sound. A horn.

"They're here," Peter yelled, a horn in his left hand. The Protectors all grabbed their weapons and pulled on their armor.

Daniel knew that this could be the day he could go home, but he also knew this could be the day he dies.

Lucien and his troops entered the valley and marched ahead towards the Protectors. Lucien was flying above his troops with Conner and Philip bound and hanging by a rope around their waists with the other end tied to one of Lucien's legs.

The Protectors assembled in formation and marched to meet the demons out in the middle of the valley. Both sides stopped marching once they were about fifty yards away from each other. Lucien flew out to the middle of the gap between the armies, and the remaining Protector Zs and Daniel walked out to meet him. Lucien descended with Conner and Philip still hanging from each of his legs. Daniel was relieved to see Conner alive.

"We don't have to fight, you know," Lucien said. "This can all be avoided if you all just follow me. Then there won't be any more pain and suffering for any of you. All of you have suffered innumerous losses all because you believe in the Son. And for what? He's not even here for you now. Join me and spare yourselves."

"You are evil, you liar!" Peter said with authority. "You want to kill us! You want to use us and then throw us away like garbage when you've used up all of us. Just like I'm sure you did with Judas."

Daniel shivered at hearing Peter's words. Daniel didn't want to be used and thrown away like that. He didn't know what had happened to Judas, but he felt sure in his spirit that he was dead.

"Whether we prevail today or not, the Son wrote our salvation before the foundations of this world were formed," Peter bellowed. "I believe in the Son!"

"I believe in the Son!" James and the others followed.

Those words were repeated several times and angered Lucien.

"So be it, Protectors," Lucien spat softly before launching himself, Conner and Philip back up into the air.

Lucien's army immediately began charging towards the Protectors.

"Remember!" Lucien roared. "You shall not kill

any Protector Z, including Daniel. Only incapacitate them. I want them to live long enough to see every one of their beloved fellow soldiers killed and no false Son returning to save them!"

"CHARGE!" Peter howled.

Daniel ran as fast as he possibly could towards Lucien's army. He was full of courage for the first time since before his parents had died. Every demon soldier that stood before Daniel fell at his sword. Daniel couldn't believe it. He felt like someone was guiding his hand at every strike.

Daniel was about to strike another demon soldier when his feet were pulled out from underneath him. Before he knew it, he was hanging upside down flying up into the air. It was Lucien. He had grabbed Daniel by his legs and launched them both up above the valley.

Up, up, up they ascended, closer and closer to the Castle of the Son. Daniel couldn't get his bearings upside down. As Lucien reached the suspended Castle, he tossed Daniel down onto one of the Castle's balconies. Daniel slid across a golden floor.

Peter and the other Protector Zs took down so many of Lucien's men, but mixed in among the demon soldiers, they also had to fight some of the Protectors from Judas' base who were still fighting with the demon army. They did their best to try to knock these soldiers out because they did not want to kill them. They wanted to restore them.

Peter engaged with one of Judas' top soldiers. The two clashed swords and appeared to be at a stalemate of strength.

"I don't want to fight you, Peter," the soldier managed through gritted teeth. "I wish I didn't agree with Judas and betray you. How can I be made whole?"

Peter disengaged with the soldier and moved his sword far out to his side, leaving himself open to attack.

"Make your mark true now, and you shall be restored," Peter said.

The soldier lifted his sword high in the air and swung it down, hitting a demon soldier just to Peter's left.

"I believe in the Son!" the soldier screamed.

Judas' remaining Protectors echoed the chant, and unlike Judas himself, they were restored.

Daniel rose to his feet within the Castle. He appeared to be in some kind of bedroom, but it all appeared vacant and unused. Before he could make sense of anything, Lucien, with Conner and Philip still bound to him, zoomed through the balcony window and tackled Daniel back through a door, pushing him out into a gigantic, cavernous hall. Daniel slid across the floor. He rushed to his feet again.

"What do you want?" Daniel asked.

"Nothing but another chance to convince you to join me," Lucien sneered as he landed with Conner and Philip on the floor on each side of him.

"Why do you think I will do that?" Daniel asked.

"Because if you don't, you are going to feel pain in a way that you haven't felt in years," Lucien said.

Lucien grabbed Conner and held him by the neck.

"If you don't join me, your friend dies," Lucien screamed.

"No!" Daniel yelled.

"Don't join him!" Conner managed to get out through Lucien's chokehold. Philip agreed with Conner.

Daniel couldn't choose. He didn't want to work for Lucien, but he also didn't want Conner to die.

"Don't, Daniel," Conner rasped. "Just let him kill me. I don't want you to fall."

Daniel remembered what Jacob said to Lucien at the abandoned base.

If I join you, I am dead, but if I join the Son, I am alive!

"I can't let him kill you!" Daniel cried.

"But you must!" Conner gasped.

"I am losing patience!" Lucien interjected. "You must choose now."

Peter had expected to see the Son arrive

triumphantly and fight Lucien, but that had not happened. As the fight raged on with Lucien's troops in the valley, Peter was discouraged at seeing so many Protectors fall. When hope seemed lost, something happened that he never expected.

As he was fighting, he saw a great light. It wasn't the Son's, light but something else. He saw it all around him, and it transported him to the balcony of the Son's castle, where he found Daniel, Lucien, Conner and Philip. He also saw the other Protector Zs were transported with him.

It didn't take long for Peter to understand what was happening.

"Don't join him, Daniel!" Peter yelled.

"Time's up!" Lucien howled.

Lucien was about to completely crush Conner's neck when he heard a voice. A deep voice.

"Leave him alone!" a man exclaimed.

"Who is that?" Daniel asked, his voice changing instantly from confident to fearful.

"The Son," Peter said in awe.

A man in dazzling white appeared and walked closer to them. The Son.

"You," Lucien growled in anger.

"Put Conner down," the Son said.

"And why would I do that?" Lucien scorned.

"Put Conner down," the Son repeated.

"As you wish," Lucien whispered.

Lucien threw Conner down to the floor and immediately impaled him in the abdomen with his sword, pinning him to the floor.

"NOOOO!!" Daniel screamed. He and the Protector Zs all instantly launched at Lucien.

Lucien withdrew his sword from Conner and readied himself for the onslaught.

The Son watched them fight, waiting. Philip, James, John, Peter, Daniel and the other Protector Zs fought Lucien with all their might, but they were no match for Lucien. He countered every attack and pushed them away like they were small children. One by one, he incapacitated them all, until only Daniel remained.

"Pathetic," Lucien spat.

Instead of attacking, Daniel readied himself in a defensive position. Lucien lunged forward, swinging his sword straight down. Daniel raised his sword to block the blow. Lucien's strike made Daniel's knees buckle. He tried to steady himself, but Lucien kept swinging the sword down repeatedly. Daniel was eventually knocked to the ground, his sword flying from his hand.

"One last chance," Lucien demanded. "Join me or die."

"I will never join you!" Daniel exclaimed, his confidence rising.

Lucien lifted his sword up high to strike Daniel.

Daniel closed his eyes. Lucien screamed in rage as he swung his sword down, but he didn't strike Daniel.

Daniel opened his eyes. Lucien had struck… the Son. Daniel saw the Son standing in front of him with His arms outstretched wide. But something was different about the Son. He was no longer covered in dazzling white light, but rather he now looked like a normal human. He fell to the floor, dead. Everyone in the room froze in shock of what just happened. How could the Son die?

"No," Peter despaired from the floor several feet away. He was near Conner, applying pressure on Conner's wound. Lucien spun around to face them and the other Protecter Zs.

"The Son is dead," Lucien bellowed. "And he died for nothing. No one can protect you now. What kind of fool sacrifices himself for another?"

Lucien turned back to Daniel, lifted his sword and was about to deliver the killing blow when a piercing white light filled the room, blinding him.

"Do you think that you can kill him, Lucien?" the Son's voice reverberated through the castle.

Lucien began swinging his sword erratically, trying to hit the source of the light.

"I thought I killed you!" Lucien screamed. "How can you beat death!?"

The blinding light subdued just enough for Lucien to finally be able to see the Son.

"I died for Daniel, and now you can't kill him because I already paid for his death myself," the Son said. "The Spirit has raised me back from the dead, and that same Spirit is now offered to all who believe in me."

"But he doesn't believe in you," Lucien accused Daniel before the Son. "He is mine."

"He is mine, not yours, and I have saved him from his mistakes," the Son said, looking into Daniel's eyes. "I have chosen him, but it is up to him to decide if he will believe it. It's up to him to choose me."

Lucien looked frightened as if for the first time he had considered this was his last day. Out of fear, Lucien ran towards the Son with all his might and tried to strike Him again, but the Son blocked it with His own sword. It flashed like lightning engulfed with the brightest flames Daniel had ever seen. The Son pushed Lucien back, struck him once with the sword directly in the chest, and killed him. Lucien was defeated.

Then the Son walked to the balcony and descended down into the Valley, and fighting alongside the remaining Protectors, destroyed all of Lucien's army. The battle was over. The Son returned to His Castle.

Chapter 29

The Son

The Son returned to the Protector Zs and Daniel, who were all gathered around Conner. He squatted down next to Conner and touched his wound, healing it instantly.

He embraced Conner and all the Protector Zs one by one, encouraging them all. Then, he turned to Daniel.

"We need to talk, don't we, Daniel?" The Son asked.

"Yes, we do," Daniel agreed.

"I know that you want me to send you home," the Son said as they walked away from the others.

"Yes, I do," Daniel confirmed. "I want Conner to come home with me, too."

"Ah, yes, Conner Matthias Higgins has his own decision to make," the Son said. "As you know, we have need for a new Protector Z to replace Judas. I believe Conner would do an excellent job protecting the citizens of Takiro. Don't you think?"

"Yes, of course," Daniel said. "But I would miss him dearly if he stayed."

"Understandably so," the Son said. "But it's no longer time for us to discuss Conner. I need to talk about something else with you. Why did you leave me?"

"What?" Daniel asked, surprised. The Son's words read like an accusation, but there was no hint of accusation in His voice.

"Why did you leave me?" the Son asked again. "Why did you stop believing me?"

"I don't know what you are talking about," Daniel answered.

"I have something for you that might help you remember," the Son said.

They had stopped near a small table. It held one item. It was a beautifully made Bible. Daniel recognized it instantly. It was Daniel's Bible. The Son handed it to him. In his hands, Daniel felt a mix of love and loss as the memories of his parents flooded his mind.

"I thought it was God's fault because He decided to let my parents die," Daniel said. "And I was so angry."

"I understand," the Son said. "None of this was ever the Father's original plan. His original plan was to be in relationship with the first Adam, walking together in the cool of the day. The only way to have a real relationship, though, is to give people a choice. The first Adam and his helper chose rebellion, and brokenness entered your world, just like it has here in Takiro. Losing loved ones is part of that brokenness. It is all under the Father's sovereignty, but it was never his original plan. Things in your world are only going to get worse before they get better, just like it has here. But I want you to take heart, because I have overcome the world. Your parents are in a place where they are happy because they believed in me, and they are waiting for you. You have the same choice before you. Pain is a part of life and can be used for good. Even in the midst of your grief for your parents, in those same moments, you can rejoice for the time you did have with them. What a blessed gift they were to you. Remember your friends on earth. They want the best for you but you resist listening to them because of your anger towards the Father. Give them a chance. Give the Bible a chance. Give me a chance."

Daniel couldn't say anything. He just felt peace.

"I want to tell you one more thing, Daniel," the Son said. "I know that you have suffered hardships, lost so much, and felt so much pain. But let me tell you my Father so loved the world that He sent me to set it right. That's what the Bible tells you. Some things from the Bible are still to come in your world, and I will be there."

"I'm sorry," Daniel said. "I believe. Help my unbelief."

"I forgive you," the Son answered.

Daniel embraced the Son.

"Are you ready for me to send you home?" the Son asked.

"Yes, but can I say goodbye first?" Daniel asked.

"Of course," the Son said.

Daniel and the Son walked back to the Protector Zs and Conner. One by one, he was embraced by each Protector Z. Daniel was full of gratitude for his time with each of them, and the feeling was mutual. Finally, Daniel came to Conner.

"You're not coming home, are you?" Daniel asked.

"I don't know," Conner said. "I've been here for so long, or at least, it's felt so long. Maybe there is more work for me to do here first."

"Conner, if this is the last time I will ever see you," Daniel said. "I just want to say that you have been such a faithful friend to me and have never given up on me even though I have been so arrogant and mean to all of you, but you never left me like that. I'm going to be that kind of friend to others when I get back."

Daniel hugged Conner, unsure when or where he might see him again.

"Time to send you home," the Son said. "And, Daniel, remember, if you follow me, I will be with you. You will still face pain in your world, but don't worry, I will be there, too."

Daniel looked at the Son, Conner and all the

Protector Zs. They all smiled back at him as he saw a great blinding light and their faces all disappeared. As soon as the light had shown, it was gone, and Daniel found himself in his bed, lying right where he had been before all of this started.

Was it really all just a dream? It felt so real. He reached for his phone on his nightstand. He saw the date. It was the next morning. What had been weeks in Takiro had all happened in a few hours of sleep.

So, it was just a dream, he thought, placing his phone back on his nightstand.

His hand touched something unfamiliar on his nightstand after he let go of his phone. He turned on his lamp and was stunned. There on the nightstand was his Bible! He grabbed it and flipped through the pages, crying and remembering his childhood with his parents. He remembered when he threw his Bible at the dirt of their graves and left it there at the cemetery. He also remembered that the Son forgave him, and that he was forgiven for every mistake he ever made, and if he believed it, the Son would always be with him.

Daniel stopped flipping through the pages of his Bible, and he landed in the book of John. His eyes were instantly drawn to John 16:33, and what he read filled his eyes with tears of joy.

"I have told you these things, so that in me you may have

peace. In this world you will have trouble. But take heart! I have overcome the world."

Epilogue

I Believe It Was

The next morning, Daniel went to Richard's house where his friends were all having a Bible study. They didn't know he would be showing up, and they all seemed shocked to see him. Daniel apologized to them and said that he had spent some time in the Word early that morning and said that he wanted to believe. They all forgave him, prayed for him, and celebrated with him.

After leaving Richard's house, Daniel had two goals: visiting his parents' graves and trying to connect with Conner. He felt anxious about the latter task. What would he even say? What if Conner hadn't really experienced any of the same things Daniel had in the dream? He decided to visit his parents first.

It had been some time since he had last visited his parents' graves. It was a painful experience every time he went there, but today was different. Today, the joy and thankfulness he felt for the time he had been given with his parents was living alongside the grief, making it less daunting to face.

Daniel took his Bible back to the place he had

thrown it down in anger. He couldn't explain how he had it back, but he was thankful, nonetheless.

After he had spent some time reflecting about his parents and thanking God for them, he turned to leave the cemetery. Something else unexplainable happened next. Conner was standing before him. They ran to each other and instantly embraced.

"You came back!" Daniel exclaimed through tears.

"After you left, I stayed in Takiro a few more days," Conner said. "I just wanted to make sure everyone was good before I left. I told the Son I wanted to come home, and then I woke up in my bed. Daniel, I had been in Takiro for years, but when I woke up, I had only been asleep for a few hours. It doesn't make any sense."

"It was the same for me," Daniel said.

"I immediately drove to my parents' house," Conner said. "I was so desperate to see them, but they were so confused. For them, they had just seen me yesterday, but for me, it had been so long. I couldn't possibly explain it to them. They would think I had lost my mind."

"Maybe we have," Daniel laughed.

"It was real, right?" Conner asked. "It had to be."

"I believe it was," Daniel said.

Daniel and Conner renewed their friendship and remained close friends for the rest of their lives.

Despite living on different coasts, they stayed in touch often and made time every year to spend time together.

Daniel continued to spend more time reading his Bible and remembering everything from the adventure of his dream. Daniel always reminded himself of the words the Son had said to him. He became devoted to his local church and soon met a woman there whom he began to love dearly. That same year, he was baptized and became a pastor. Soon, Daniel was married and began to create a family with his wife. They had three children: Rhys, Elisha and Eden.

Daniel was forever changed after his adventure in Takiro. His faith had turned from nothing to solid as a rock.

Author's Note

Just like in my first book, The Dino Life, we meet a character who has lost loved ones, but instead of holding strong in his faith, he let go of it and left his creator. Daniel suffered a lot and didn't know how to handle it. Conner is the friend who wants to help him come back to God and never gives up on him. I want all of you readers to know and remember how much God truly cares and loves you. Life is hard, and losing people you love is part of it, but God is in control of it all. If you believe in what Jesus did on the cross, repent and turn away from evil and confess that He is Lord, you will be with Him for eternity.

Never forget God's constant love.

"This is how God showed his love among us: He sent his one and only Son into the world that we might live through him. This is love: not that we loved God, but that he loved us and sent his Son as an atoning sacrifice for our sins." 1 John 4:9-10

About the Author

Canaan Gilbert lives in Arkansas with his Mom, Dad, and his little brother and sister. This is his second book. He is a member of New Life Church with his family. He is very excited for several more books he is going to publish. Subscribe to the SUPER GILBERT BROS. channel on YouTube to see Canaan, his brother, and his sister play games, give reviews on movies, and more!

"If I join you, I am dead, but if I join the Son, I am alive!"
- Jacob the Faithful

Made in the USA
Columbia, SC
15 November 2024